CALICO ILLUSTRATED CLASSICS

Robert Louis Stevenson's

KIDNAPPED

ADAPTED BY: Jan Fields
ILLUSTRATED BY: Eric Scott Fisher

magic
Wagon

Published by Magic Wagon, a division of the ABDO Group,
8000 West 78th Street, Edina, Minnesota 55439. Copyright
© 2011 by Abdo Consulting Group, Inc. International copyrights
reserved in all countries. All rights reserved. No part of this
book may be reproduced in any form without written permission
from the publisher.

Calico Chapter Books™ is a trademark and logo of Magic Wagon.

Printed in the United States of America, Melrose Park, Illinois.
102010
012011
This book contains at least 10% recycled materials.

Original text by Robert Louis Stevenson
Adapted by Jan Fields
Illustrated by Eric Scott Fisher
Edited by Stephanie Hedlund and Rochelle Baltzer
Cover and interior design by Abbey Fitzgerald

Library of Congress Cataloging-in-Publication Data

Fields, Jan.
  Kidnapped / Robert Louis Stevenson ; adapted by Jan Fields ;
illustrated by Eric Scott Fisher.
    p. cm. -- (Calico illustrated classics)
  ISBN 978-1-61641-105-3
  1. Scotland--History--18th century--Juvenile fiction. [1. Scotland-
-History--18th century--Fiction. 2. Adventure and adventurers-
-Fiction. 3. Coming of age--Fiction.] I. Fisher, Eric Scott, ill. II.
Stevenson, Robert Louis, 1850-1894. Kidnapped. III. Title.
  PZ7.F479177Ki 2011
  [Fic]--dc22
                                        2010031042

Table of Contents

I Set Off

My adventure began on a morning in June 1751, when I took the key from the door of my father's house for the last time. The sun lit the hills as I walked down the road. Blackbirds whistled in the garden lilacs.

Our local minister waited for me by the garden gate. Mr. Campbell shook my hand. "Well, Davey," he said, "are you sorry to leave Essendean?"

"I have been happy here," I said. "But I have never been anywhere else. With my father and mother dead, I don't know where to go."

"Your father gave me a letter and told me to give it to you after he was gone. He said to send you to the house of Shaws. It lies not far from the town of Cramond."

I stared dumbly. My father had never spoken of a connection with any wealthy landowners. "What had my poor father to do with the house of Shaws?"

"I do not know. But the name on the letter suggests you may have family there." The minister handed me the letter and I saw that it was addressed to Ebenezer Balfour. My heart beat fast as I stared at it. I sensed adventure in my hands.

"I am not sure what I should do," I stammered.

"I think you should go," he said. Then he gave me the money gained from selling my father's books, along with small gifts from him and his wife. He clapped me on my back and sent me on my way.

I was glad to set out. When I reached the Glasgow road on my second day, I spied a regiment marching in time to the sound of a fife. At the sight of the red coats and merry music, I felt a swelling pride.

Soon after that I reached Cramond parish. I began to ask how to find the house of Shaws. My question seemed to surprise everyone I asked. Several people even warned me away from going closer.

With each warning, I felt more and more nervous. Where exactly was I going? I stopped a cart driver and asked if he knew of the house. He did.

"It's a big, shambling house," he said. "But there are no folks there."

"What?" I asked. "Not Mr. Ebenezer?"

"Oh, aye," said the man. "The Laird is there, if it's him you're wanting. You seem a decent lad. If you'll take a word from me, you'll stay clear of the Shaws."

He would say no more, but went on his way. I was tempted to abandon my adventure, but I had come so far already. Though I slowed down a bit, I kept on my way.

Close to sundown I met a sour-looking woman trudging down a hill. When I asked her

my question, she led me back up the hill and pointed to the great bulk of a building standing very bare at the bottom of the next valley.

The valley was beautiful, with low hills and good crops, but the house seemed to be in ruins. No road led to it. No smoke rose from a chimney. There was no sign of a garden. My heart sank.

"That is the house of Shaws!" the woman cried. "Blood built it. Blood will bring it down." Then the woman turned with surprising speed and hurried away.

I sat down and stared at the house of Shaws. Country folk passed by me as I sat, but I lacked the spirit to speak to them. Finally when the sun went down, I saw the slightest wisp of smoke coming from the ruin of the house. This comforted me a bit, and I set forward to reach my destination.

The nearer I got to the house, the drearier it looked. One wing of the house seemed half finished. I could see steps and stairs and uncompleted masonry. The house was dotted with broken windows where bats flew in and out.

Finally, I reached the door. I knocked once and waited. No response. I knocked again and then again. I grew angry and began to kick the door. I shouted for Mr. Balfour. Finally I heard a sound overhead. A man leaned out of a first story window with a blunderbuss.

"It's loaded," he said.

"I have come with a letter for Mr. Ebenezer Balfour of the Shaws. Is he here? I am David Balfour."

At that, the man jumped and I heard the blunderbuss rattle in the windowsill. Finally he asked, "Is your father dead?"

I was so surprised at this question that I didn't answer and only stood staring.

"Aye, he must be dead or why would you be at my door. I'll let you in." And he disappeared from the window.

My Uncle

I heard a great rattle of chains and bolts, and the door opened slowly. It shut quickly behind me as soon as I stepped within.

"Go into the kitchen and touch nothing," a gravelly voice spoke from the darkness. I heard the sound of chains and locks again behind me as I groped my way forward in the dark.

A fire burned in the kitchen, and I could see the room was nearly empty. A few dishes stood upon a shelf. A small table held a bowl of porridge, a spoon, and a cup. There was not one other thing in that large, empty room except a row of chests and a single padlocked cupboard on the wall.

The old man shuffled in, wearing a loose flannel nightshirt. He was thin and bent with gray skin. I could not guess at his age. He might have been 50 or 70. He would not look at me directly, but I had the sense that he watched me from the corner of his eye. I guessed him to be the servant of the man I sought.

"You can eat the porridge if you're hungry," he said.

"I don't want to take your supper," I said.

"I can do fine without it, but I'll take my cup. A bit of something to drink eases my cough." He drank from the cup, his eyes still following me. He held out his hand. "Let me see the letter."

"The letter is for Mr. Balfour," I said. "I would prefer to give it to him."

"And who do you think I am?" he snapped, shaking the hand that he still held out. "Give me Alexander's letter."

"You know my father's name?"

"It would be strange if I didn't know my brother's name. I am your uncle and you are my nephew. So give me the letter, sit down, and eat."

I felt bitter disappointment at the thought of this man being my uncle. I stared into the bowl of cooling porridge but had little interest in it. My uncle turned the letter over and over in his hands.

"You know what this says?" he asked.

"You can see that the seal was never broken," I replied, growing angry at his tone.

"I expect you have hopes for money from me," he grumbled.

"I am no beggar. I have friends who will cheerfully help me."

"Now calm down. We can come to an agreement." He peered directly at the untouched bowl of porridge now and asked if I intended to eat it.

I got up and he took my place at the table. I stood stiffly as my uncle gobbled the porridge. When he finished, he looked at me again. "Your father has been long dead?"

"Three weeks, sir."

"And he never spoke of me, or of the Shaws?"

"Never."

At that the old man seemed to cheer up considerably. "We'll get along fine yet," he said. "I'll show you a bed." To my surprise, he lit no light and we wandered through pitch dark corridors groping our way along. Finally, he opened the door and urged me in with a hand on my arm.

"Can I have a light?" I asked.

"There is light enough," he answered, though there was neither moon nor star in the cloudy sky through the window. "I don't allow candles in my house. I'm terribly afraid of fire. Good night."

Before I had time for another word, he pulled the door closed. I heard him lock me in. I didn't know whether to laugh or cry.

The room was damp and cold. I felt around and found the bed, which was soggy. Finally, I lay on the floor with my bundle as a pillow and my plaid as a blanket. I fell quickly asleep.

When morning came, I could see what a miserable room it truly was. Many of the window panes were broken. Mold had taken over every bit of furniture.

I banged on my door and shouted until my uncle let me out. He led me outside to a well and suggested I wash up. When I went to the kitchen I found two bowls of porridge, two spoons, but only one cup.

I mentioned that I would like to have a drink as well. My uncle fetched a second cup and divided the contents of the first in two.

After we had finished our meal, my uncle asked about my mother. He actually seemed sad to hear she was dead as well. Then he asked about the friends I had mentioned. I told him of Mr. Campbell and spoke vaguely of others. I confess my extra friends were more imaginary than true, but I did not want him to think me helpless.

"I will do right by you, Davey," he said. "But as I decide how best to do that, I'd not like to be talked about to your Campbell friends. So you'll not be sending any messages while you're in this house."

"If you want me out of your house, you need only say so," I said. "I have no interest in forcing anything on you."

"I only ask that you stay a day or two, without spreading tales of me. I promise you'll be glad you did."

I told my uncle that if I stayed, I would need a better bed without quite so much swamp in it.

"Is this my house or yours?" he snapped, then immediately changed his tone. "I didn't mean that. I'm sure we can make your bed comfortable." At that, my uncle said he needed to go out. "I can't leave you by yourself in the house. I'll have to lock you out."

At that, my anger rose hot in my face. "If you lock me out, it'll be the last you see of me in friendship."

He turned very pale and glared. We stared at one another for a moment and he finally smiled. "Well, we must make compromises for family. I'll just stay home."

"Uncle Ebenezer," I said, "you treat me like a thief. You behave as if you hate me. Why would you want me to stay? I'll just go home and seek my future differently."

At this, Uncle Ebenezer grew very earnest. "I like you just fine. We will agree. I don't want you to go. Stay a little while and you'll be glad you did."

Great Danger

The day passed fairly well. We had cold porridge at noon and hot porridge at night. Apparently porridge was all my uncle ate. He spoke very little. I found piles of books in the one small room he allowed me to enter. I was able to pass the day looking through the books.

In one small book of poetry, I found an inscription, "To my brother Ebenezer on his fifth birthday." It was signed by my father. This puzzled me. If my father was the younger brother, how could he write such a clear inscription when less than five years old?

As I settled down across from my uncle for supper, I chanced to ask him if he and my father were twins. He jumped up, dropping his spoon. He grabbed the breast of my jacket and peered into my eyes. "What makes you ask that?"

I calmly told him to take his hands from my jacket and control himself. He did, and sank back down upon his stool, blinking at his porridge.

"You shouldn't speak to me about your father. He was the only brother I ever had."

I began to wonder if my uncle were insane and possibly dangerous. I also suspected all the stronger that Uncle Ebenezer was not the elder brother. With this notion strongly in my head, my uncle and I cut sharp glances at one another through the rest of the meal.

Finally my uncle said, "I don't want you to think I'm a miserly man. I will be happy to share with you a bit to get you started on your way. Forty pounds. Just step outside that I might gather it."

I did, standing in the dark night with the wind moaning around the house. Finally, my uncle called me back in and counted out the money as if each coin were cut from his beating heart.

"There," he gasped at the end. "That will show that my word is my bond! I'm pleased to do right by my brother's son. Now I wonder if you might do me a favor."

He pulled a key from one of his pockets. "There is a chest of papers I need," he said, thrusting the key at me. "They are in a tower room up the stairs in the rough part of the house. I'm a bit broken and not so good with the stairs."

I frowned but asked, "Are the stairs good?"

"They're grand," he said eagerly. "Keep to the wall though, as there are no banisters."

"Can I have a light?" I asked.

He shook his head and shuddered. "Not in my house. The fire!"

The stairs could only be reached from outside, so I stepped out in the black night. The wind moaned in the distance. I had to feel my way along the wall to reach the tower door.

The tower was dark, and I felt for the first stair with foot and hand. The steps were steep and narrow but felt solid underfoot. I kept close to the tower wall and felt my way in the pitch darkness with a pounding heart.

The house of Shaws stood a five full stories high not counting lofts. As I crept upward, the stair grew airier. Lightning flashed then and lit the tower for a moment. I saw that the stairs were uneven widths and my foot was within two inches of a steep drop to the ground.

I got down on hands and knees then to continue up the stairs, feeling before me every inch. The flash of lightning had disturbed the tower bats and they flocked downward, beating about my face and body.

The stairs turned in a corkscrew as they climbed the tower, and it seemed the turns grew sharper as I climbed. I had come to one of these turns and felt forward as usual. My hand slipped upon an edge and found nothing beyond it.

The stair went no higher. Had I been walking up the stairs, I would have stepped into the next life. No one could have survived the fall. The thought of how close I had come to death made me break out in a sweat and shake.

I slowly groped my way back down the steps. The wind sprang up and shook the tower. The rain followed, falling in buckets by the time I reached the ground.

I looked along the wall toward the kitchen and saw a light. The kitchen door was open and I saw a figure in the doorway, looking out into the storm.

Lightning brightened the scene like daylight and I saw my uncle clearly. A hard crash of thunder followed, and he jumped and ran back into the house.

I crept into the kitchen behind him and cried, "Ah!"

My uncle gave a bleat of terror and tumbled to the floor like a dead man. I retrieved his keys, thinking to find a way to arm myself before he roused himself again. In the locked cupboards I found bags of meal and bags of money. I also found clothes and an ugly Highland dirk with no scabbard. This I hid in my coat before turning back to my uncle.

He seemed to be waking. "Come," I said. "Sit up."

"Are you alive?" he sobbed.

"That I am," I said. "Small thanks to you."

He asked me to give him some medicine for his heart and I fetched it. As I raised him up to drink the medicine, I asked why he had tried to kill me.

"I'll tell you in the morning," he gasped. "As sure as death I will."

So that night it was I who locked him in his room. Then, I made a bed up beside the kitchen fire and slept.

CHAPTER
4
Queen's Ferry

The next morning, a winter wind blew out of the northwest and drove the clouds away. Though my uncle had showed his plans for me, I still felt no fear. I was certain I could best him.

I let the old man out of his room. He tried to pretend my trip up the stairs was some kind of joke, but he soon saw I was unlikely to accept that for a moment.

Suddenly we were interrupted by a knock on the door. I found a half-grown boy shaking in the cold.

"What cheer, mate?" he asked with a cracked voice.

"What business have you here?" I asked.

"I brought a letter from the captain to Mr. Belflower." He showed me a letter as he spoke. "And I'm very hungry."

"Come into the house and have a bite to eat," I said.

My uncle read the letter and then handed it to me. It was from a ship's captain with whom my uncle had done business in the past.

"This man Hoseason is the captain of a trading ship called *Covenant*. I need to meet with him. If you come along with me, we can stop at the lawyer's afterward. Mr. Rankeillor is a fine lawyer and knew your father. We'll settle what's rightly yours proper and legal."

I stood a while in thought. I liked the idea of seeing the dock and was certain my frail uncle could hardly overpower me on the road.

"Very well," I said. "Let us go."

My uncle got his hat and coat and buckled on an old rusty cutlass. We put out the fire, locked the door, and set forth. Though it was

June, it might as well have been winter so cold was the wind in our faces. Uncle Ebenezer never said a word the whole way.

The cabin boy was eager to chat. I learned his name was Ransome. His life at sea was filled with beatings at the hands of the captain and the navigator, Mr. Shuan. The boy proudly showed me scars and raw wounds to prove his beatings.

"You are no slave to be so ill treated," I said, outraged. "Why do you stay?"

"What should I do?" the boy said scornfully. "Grub around in the dirt? Go to school?" He said school with a kind of horror.

It quickly became clear that despite the boy's ill use, he truly believed the sea was the best place to be. And he had great pride in being aboard the *Covenant*. He told there was no greater moment than to come ashore with money in his pocket that he had earned himself.

Finally we came to the top of the hill and looked down upon the water. The Firth of

Forth narrows at this point to the width of a good-sized river, which makes it a convenient haven for ships. Near the pier I saw a building which they call the Hawes Inn.

The boy pointed out the *Covenant* anchored about a half-mile offshore. After his gruesome stories of abuse, I shuddered at the sight of the ship.

"There's nothing that would get me aboard that *Covenant*," I said.

"If you say so, then we have to please you," my uncle said. "We'll meet the captain at the inn."

The captain's room at the inn was stifling hot. The captain said it was a habit he had picked up while sailing in the tropics. When my uncle suggested I run along downstairs and look at the pier, I was fool enough to go just to get out of the heat.

The air smelled of salt. As I watched, the hands aboard the *Covenant* were beginning to shake out her sails. I looked at the seamen aboard the ship skiff that was tied to the pier. They were big, brown fellows with colored handkerchiefs about the throats. The scent and sights made me imagine far voyages and foreign places.

Ransome walked at my side and pointed out different things along the way. I asked him if he knew of the lawyer Mr. Rankeillor.

"Aye," he said. "He's a good and honest man. Which I have not heard said of Mr. Ebenezer."

This didn't surprise me at all. By this point we'd reached the inn again and the innkeeper overheard the last of our conversation.

"I heard Ebenezer killed his own brother," the innkeeper said. "You look a bit like Mr. Alexander."

"What would Ebenezer kill him for?" I asked.

"Just to get the place," the man said.

"So Alexander was the eldest son?"

The innkeeper nodded. "Indeed he was."

Having my suspicions set out right still stunned me with my good fortune. Not two days ago I was a poor lad, and now I had a house in broad lands.

As I thought on this, I spotted Captain Hoseason marching toward me. He was a tall man with as a serious expression on his face. He put his arm around me and whispered in my ear, "Be careful of the old man. I believe he means you ill. Come aboard with me so we can talk."

I did not dream of hanging back. I thought I had found a good friend and helper. I was eager to see the ship and to hear the captain's advice.

When my feet were on deck, I felt dizzy with the unsteadiness of everything around me. I turned to the captain and said, "Now, what of my uncle?"

The captain looked at me grimly. "What of him? That's the point."

I pulled clear of him and ran for the rail. "Help, help! Murder!" I could see my uncle on the pier. Strong hands pulled me away from the ship's rail. I saw a great flash of light and fell senseless.

CHAPTER 5

The Covenant

I awoke in pain and darkness. I heard a roar of water, the thrashing of heavy spray against the ship, and the shouts of men. My stomach rolled and hurled. I could find no place of comfort, as my hands and feet were bound.

Day and night were alike in the ship's bowels where I lay. I have no idea how long I traveled that way before I was awakened by a lantern in my face and voices close by.

"See for yourself, sir," the first voice said. "He has a high fever. I want the boy taken out of this hole and put in the forecastle."

"What you want is of no concern of mine," a second voice answered. This one I recognized as Captain Hoseason. "He is fine here."

"I was paid to be second officer of this ship," the other man said. "But I was not paid enough to be party to murder."

"Murder!" the captain roared. "What kind of talk is that?"

"Talk you can understand," the other man said. "Leave the boy here and he will die."

"Then take him where you please," the captain grumbled. He turned and climbed the ladder.

The mate bent over me then. He was a small man of about thirty with green eyes and a tangle of fair hair.

"Cheer up," he said. "We'll make you well soon enough." He cut my bonds then, and I felt myself hoisted onto a man's back just before I lost my senses again.

I awoke in a narrow bunk in the forecastle. Men lounged around or slept. One of the men brought me a drink of something healing. The first mate, Riach, visited regularly to check on me.

"A little knock on the head won't keep you down long," Riach said cheerily. "It was me that gave it to you!"

And so I lay for days, recovering and getting to know the ship's hands. They were a rough lot but kind when it occurred to them. Moreover, they were simple and direct. They even returned my money, which they had divided up when I was first captured.

I learned we were heading for the Carolinas, where I would be sold as a slave on the plantations. I saw Ransome with fresh bruises on his arm. He raved against the navigator, Mr. Shuan. I complained that the boy's mistreatment was horrendous, but the crew admired Shuan greatly. Apparently he was the only true seaman aboard the ship.

Riach visited me often and I told him my whole story. He offered to pass along letters to Mr. Campbell and Mr. Rankeillor if I wished.

They might be able to help me once I reached my destination.

"You never know where the wind will blow you. Look at me," he said. "I'm a laird's son and here I am!"

During all this time, the *Covenant* was barely creeping along against constant headwinds. The mood of the sailors grew restless and gruff. Though I thought we must be halfway across the Atlantic, we were barely into the high sea between the Orkney and Shetland Islands.

Then one night, the captain walked into the forecastle and spoke to me. "We want you to serve as cabin boy in the roundhouse. You'll change berths with Ransome."

As he spoke, two seamen carried Ransome into the forecastle. The boy's small face was white as wax and he never moved. I gasped at the sight.

"Run away aft with you," Hoseason ordered.

The roundhouse stood some six feet above the decks. Inside, a fixed table with a bench took up the center of the room. The walls were fitted with lockers from top to bottom. Two bunks served as sleeping quarters for the captain and the mates, as at least one man was on deck at all times. A storeroom lay underneath the floor and held the best of the ship's food store and all of the firearms.

Shuan sat at the table, staring blankly. He took no notice of my coming in. When the captain and Riach came into the roundhouse, I knew by their faces that the boy had died.

"You've murdered the boy," the captain said to the blank-faced navigator.

"He brought me a dirty cup," the man said, then began crying soundlessly. The captain led him across to his bunk and told him to sleep.

"The boy died at sea," the captain. "That's all we'll say about it." Then he sat down to the table and called me to wait on him.

In the few days ahead, I waited on the three men whenever they wanted something. I slept on the floor of the roundhouse and rarely had more than scant hours without being awakened to serve. Still, the men were not unkind to me with poor Ransome so heavy on everyone's hearts.

CHAPTER
6

The Man with the Gold Belt

During the next week, the winds and currents grew worse. Some days the *Covenant* was actually beaten backward toward the south. Finally, the officers decided to make a fair wind of a foul one and run south instead of north.

Then one night as I was serving Riach and the captain a late supper, the ship struck something with a great sound.

We rushed to the deck. "She's struck!" Riach cried.

"No, sir," the captain answered. "We've only run a boat down."

We had struck a boat in the fog, breaking it in two. It sank with all aboard except one man, who had been flung well clear of the boat.

He was hauled aboard and brought into the roundhouse.

He was a smallish man but nimble as a goat. His skin was burnt very dark and heavily freckled. His eyes were light and danced with something like madness, making him both engaging and alarming. He wore a pair of silver pistols and a great sword. I felt sure he would make a dangerous enemy.

The captain spoke with the man, but it was difficult to sort out what manner of conversation it was. Each seemed to talk around what he would say.

Finally, the stranger said, "I'll be plain. I am an honest man. I say only the line of King James are the true kings. I've had to spend a fair bit of time in France for my own safety. I would like to return there. I can reward you highly for your trouble."

"I cannot carry you to France," the captain said. "But I might return you to the Scottish shore."

The gentleman took a money belt from about his waist and poured gold guineas on the table. The captain's eyes grew wide. "Half of that," he said, "and I'm your man."

"That money isn't mine to give," the stranger said. "It belongs to my chieftain and is a gift from his clan. He would agree that I could give a small bit so that the rest reaches him safely."

"And if I turn you over to the soldiers?" the captain asked.

"Then the soldiers of King George will take every guinea and you'll have none," the man said.

The captain finally settled on sixty guineas to transport the stranger safely. They shook hands on it, and the captain hurried out.

I assumed the stranger had been exiled as a supporter of the Stuart line for Scottish rule. Returning to Scotland would mean his arrest and death.

I set a plate of dinner before him and said, "So you're a Jacobite?"

"And you would be a Whig?" he asked.

"As good a Whig as my local minister could make me," I said lightly. The difference between Jacobites and Whigs went deeper than who they supported for king. The Jacobites were also Catholic, while the Whigs were Protestant like King George.

"Well, good Whig," he said lightly. "Could I get something to drink with my meal?"

"I'll go and get the key," I said, since everything except water was locked up under our feet. As I crossed the deck, I saw the fog was still thick. It hid me from the officers until I was well upon them. I paused as I heard them speak.

"Should we lure him out of the roundhouse first?" Riach asked.

"No," the captain answered. "The tight quarters will make it harder for him to use his sword."

I stepped out of the fog then and asked for the key to the stores.

"Ah, here's our chance to get to the firearms," the captain said, clapping me on the back. "That wild Highlander is a danger to the ship, David. But our firearms are locked in the roundhouse. You could snap up a pistol or two without his notice." He handed me the keys and sent me back toward the roundhouse.

I debated all the way back. Which side should I defend? I had not been able to stop the murder of poor Ransome, and now they wanted my hand in the killing of this Highlander. Did I want to be party to such?

Finally I rushed into the roundhouse, almost gasping. "They're all murderers here. They've killed a boy already, and now it's you they're after."

"They haven't got me yet," the man said, as he sprang to his feet. "Will you stand with me?"

"I will."

He asked my name and I told him David Balfour of Shaws, claiming my inheritance in word.

"My name is Stewart," he said, drawing himself up. "Alan Breck, they call me. I have no land to clap on the end of it, but I have the name of a king and that's enough."

We cast open the hold and retrieved the pistols. I was to load them and watch for attack through the rear door and the skylight.

"If they try to knock down the door, shoot them," he said. "And if you hear the breaking of the skylight glass, shoot them there. I will deal with all who come at the other door."

The Siege

The officers on deck grew impatient waiting on my return. The captain appeared at the open door.

"Stand!" Breck cried, pointing his sword.

"This is a strange return for hospitality," the captain said, giving me an ugly look as I sat loading pistols. "David, I'll mind this." Then he disappeared from the door.

"Keep your head," Breck said. "It's coming."

I climbed up on the berth and kept watch. I heard a clash of steel and knew the officers must be handing out swords. I wondered if this would be one of the last moments of my life.

Then I heard a rush and a roar. I looked toward the open door and saw Shuan crossing blades with Breck.

"That's him that killed the boy," I shouted.

"Look to your windows," Breck replied.

I had scarce turned back to my window before five men carrying a battering ram made a run for the back door. I had never fired a pistol in my life but I cried, "Take that!" and shot into their midst.

My shot struck the captain and he staggered back a step. I sent another ball over their heads, and my third shot went wide as well. The men threw down the battering ram and ran for it.

The air around me was full of smoke from my own firing. Breck stood at the door, his sword running blood up to the hilt. He looked invincible. Shuan lay just outside the door but then vanished as some of the other crewmen dragged him away by the ankles.

"I've settled two," Breck said.

"I winged the captain," I offered.

"We're not done yet," he said. "They'll be back. To your watch!"

I settled back to my place and reloaded the guns I had fired. I could hear our enemies disputing not far off upon the deck. I heard one man say Shuan was dead.

Then I heard stealthy footsteps creeping along Breck's side of the roundhouse. I knew he wasn't likely to have missed the sounds. Next I heard someone drop softly on the roof above me.

A single whistle on the sea pipe rang out and the knot of them made one rush of it against the door. At the same moment, the glass of the skylight shattered and a man leaped through and landed on the floor.

Before he could stand, I clapped the barrel of the pistol against his back. He spun around and jumped at me. I shot him then and he gave a horrible groan before crumpling to the floor.

Another man's leg appeared above me through the skylight. I shot him through the thigh.

At the door, Breck's sword flashed like quicksilver as he drove the attacking sailors back like a sheepdog drives sheep. The second battle was over.

"David," he cried, "I love you like a brother!" He tumbled the fallen men out the door, humming to himself all the while. I soon realized he was composing a song about himself and his fighting. I noticed I wasn't mentioned in the tune at all.

With the room cleared, Breck said, "I'll take the first watch." So I laid down in my usual place on the floor and slept.

I awoke to a quiet morning with only rain drumming against the roundhouse. I could hear the helm banging, which meant no one was at the tiller. Indeed, the battle had left so many hurt that the ship had drifted very near the coast. I looked out the door and saw the great stone hills of Skye on the right.

CHAPTER
8
Victory

Breck and I sat down to breakfast not long after dawn. The floor was covered with broken glass and blood, which took away my hunger.

"We'll hear from them before long," Breck said cheerfully. Then he took a knife from the table and cut a silver button from his coat. "These came from my father, Duncan Stewart. I give you one as a keepsake for last night's work. If you have a need, show this button and the friends of Alan Breck will come around you."

I fought a smile at the grand way he pronounced this, as if he had armies of men at his call. Breck stayed busy cleaning up his fine coat as best he could. He was still at this task when the crew called for a parley. We agreed.

The captain came close to one of the windows, and Breck held a pistol in his face.

"Have I not given my word?" the captain roared. "Or do you seek to insult me with that thing?"

"I've not had good experience with your word," Breck reminded him.

"Well, you've done a fine job at robbing me of crew," the captain said. "I have no choice but to put into port at Glasgow and seek more. You may exit there."

"No," Breck said. "You'll take me ashore where we agreed."

The captain shook his head. "Isn't possible. I barely have enough healthy men to sail. My navigator is dead, and no other can guide us on this coast."

"Well, land me safely from King George's soldiers and I'll pay you," Breck said finally. "I'll help guide you where I can. I've been on this shore times enough."

With nothing else to do, Breck asked me about my life. I told him about my good friend Mr. Campbell, the minister. He cried out that he hated every man who wore the name Campbell.

"Our minister is as fine a man as you could give your hand to," I insisted. "What is your problem with the Campbells?"

"I've told you I'm an Appin Stewart," Breck said. "The Campbells have long abused and robbed the Stewarts. But my father was a fine man. King George once gave him three gold guineas in admiration for his skill as a swordsman. My father gave the guineas to a manservant to show the kind of Highland gentleman he was."

"Sounds like he was not the kind of gentleman to leave you rich," I noticed. Breck laughed, admitting that was true.

"That's why I enlisted," Breck said.

I gaped at him. "You were in the English army?"

"For a time," he said. "It didn't suit me, but that's why it would be best if I didn't meet any red coats."

"So you are an army deserter, a condemned rebel, and you secretly gather gold for exiled clansmen," I summed up. "Why would you come anywhere near this country again? Do you have a death wish?"

"I missed my friends and country," Breck said. "And I come to collect money to help the leader of our clan. My people are staunch. King George tries to starve them with rent, but they still scrape up money for our clan captain Ardshiel. My kinsman James Stewart is Ardshiel's half brother. He collects the money and I carry it to our chief in exile."

"That sounds noble," I said.

"You're a gentleman then, even if you are a Whig," Breck said cheerfully. "You'd be ashamed of the suffering my people has had. They cast a man in jail for wearing a kilt or a tartan plaid. They've taken every weapon from the hands of our people. And the worst of the Campbells is the Red Fox."

"The Red Fox?" I echoed.

"Colin Roy Campbell. He's King George's hand on the lands of Appin. When he heard tell that our people were sending money to support the chief in exile, he decided to run our clan off the land. If he ever comes my way, I'll end his days on this earth."

"It's not wise to nurse so much anger," I advised.

Breck snorted. "It would be a convenient world if we all followed your Whig ways and let men like Colin Roy trample our families into the ground." He shook his head at me. "You're a good man in a fight, David, but you've got odd notions."

Then Breck fell sad and silent for a long while.

Shipwrecked

Night fell and Captain Hoseason clapped his head into the roundhouse door. "Come out and see if you can pilot," he called to Breck. "My ship's in danger."

One look at his face made it plain he was deadly serious. Breck and I hurried out on deck. The sky was clear with a bitter cold wind that pushed the *Covenant* through the seas at a great rate. The full moon was bright enough to show the southwest corner of the Island of Mull.

The captain pointed off the side where a thing like a fountain rose out of the moonlit sea. "That sea is breaking on a reef," Breck said.

"Aye," the captain agreed. "And so will we. Without Shuan or a chart, I've no way of dodging them."

Breck nodded. "It's the Torran Rocks. There are ten miles of them. I'm no pilot, but I believe the safest route is close to land."

So the captain ordered the ship in as close to the shoreline as they dared. It was soon clear that Breck was right. The rocks were fewer as we crept along the shore. The crew watched sharp for the sight of the reef spouts and sang out so that we could dodge them.

I noticed Breck had grown white as milk during this tense game of watching and dodging. Suddenly the tide caught the brig and threw the wind out of her sails. She came round into the wind like a top, and the next moment struck a reef so hard it threw us all to the deck.

Thus caught, the ship began to beat herself to pieces against the rocks. The crew scrambled for the skiff to abandon ship.

There followed a wave so huge that it lifted the ship right up and canted her over on her beam. At the sudden tilting of the ship, I was cast clean over the bulwarks into the sea.

I went under, came up coughing, and went under again. Over and over, I bobbed as the sea battered me. Each time it pushed me under, I expected to stay. Then I caught hold of a piece of the ship, broken and floating. I rode the sea better then. The waves pushed me into quieter water.

I spied the shores of Earraid and felt sure I must reach them before I froze to death. I gripped the broken bit of spar tighter and kicked. For an hour I kicked and splashed until I reached water so shallow that I could leave my bit of ship behind and wade ashore upon my feet.

I dared not lay down and sleep, for I was sure I would freeze. I paced and pounded my chest to fight the cold. I heard no sound beyond the sea. When the sun rose, I looked out across the water and saw no sign of ship or shipmates.

I walked over my small islet and found neither food, nor shelter, nor fresh water. I discovered that the small islet lay close to a larger bit of land that showed signs of habitation, but a strait lay between me and it.

I tried to wade across the narrowest bit but was soon in over my head, and I was no swimmer. I struggled back to shore. I wept for the foolishness of letting my little scrap of boat drift away. I could have used it to cross the strait just as I had used it to reach the islet.

I found shellfish among the rocks of the isle and this is all I ate while I spent my miserable time there. Sometimes they set well on my stomach, and sometimes they left me gagging and weak from throwing them back up.

Rain poured down and there was no dry place to be found. I slept between two rocks that kept my face dry but left my feet in a bog. I watched the shores of the larger island and spied smoke curling from chimneys. How could I be so close to warmth and food but unable to reach it?

On the morning of the third day, I saw a buck with a fine spread of antlers standing on a tall rock of the islet. I supposed he must have swum the strait, though I could not imagine what would have drawn him to my islet. With no weapon, the deer did me no good.

In books, whenever someone is cast ashore, they always have all manner of useful tools for finding food and building shelter. I had wet clothes and a silver button. I had even lost most of my money. It must have been washed from my pockets by the sea.

Then on the fourth day, I spotted a small boat coming toward me. I raced to the shore's edge and waved my arms. As soon as they were within easy speech, they let down their sail and lay quiet. In spite of my calling out to them, they drew no nearer.

One man called out to me, speaking fast in Gaelic and waving his hands. I called out that I could not understand him as I did not speak Gaelic. He seemed angry at that and spoke even more quickly. I caught a word several times that sounded like, "whateffer," and realized he was trying to speak English.

I called back, "Whatever."

He grinned and looked at his companion as if proud of his skills. Then he spoke another rattle of words and I picked out "tide."

"Tide?" I called.

He waved his arms down toward the end of the islet that was bordered by the strait.

"Tide!" I yelped.

I turned then and ran for the strait. In about a half hour, I reached it and discovered that the deep water had shrunk to a trickle with the outgoing tide. I could easily walk across to the main island.

I felt very foolish to realize I need not have spent a day on the little islet. I picked my way up the rocky shore, certain that any youth from an adventure story had more sense than I would ever hope for.

CHAPTER 10

The Silver Button

I was now standing on the Ross of Mull, which seemed nearly as rugged as the tiny islet I had just escaped. I aimed as well as I could for the smoke I had seen from my little islet and reached the house by early evening.

It was built of piled stone and set long and low with a turf roof. An old man sat in front smoking a pipe. We talked with what little English he had. He knew of my shipmates and had fed them when they came ashore, more quickly and safely than I.

"Was there one dressed like a gentleman?" I asked.

He said there was, though the rest wore sailor's trousers. Then he grinned and cried out that I must be the lad with the silver button.

"Why, yes," I said.

"Then I have a word for you," he said. "Your friend said to follow him to his country by Torosay and take the ferry."

He asked how I had fared and I told him, expecting him to laugh at my foolishness. Instead, he took me by the hand and led me into his hut. I met his wife, who set food before me straightaway.

As I sat in the smoky house where light shone through as many holes as a colander, I felt I had found a palace. The good people made me a pallet on the floor and I slept through noon the next day. When I took to the road, I felt my health much improved from the sad shape I'd been in when I waded across the strait.

The old gentleman would take no money for his kindness and insisted on giving me a hat to shield my head on my travels. All my life I had heard of the wild, rough Highlanders, but as I walked, I wished I knew more of such wildness in my own neighbors.

As I walked, I saw people trying to coax crops from rocks and bogs or tending straggling groups of shaggy cows. Each person's dress seemed odder than the last.

I knew the Highland kilt was outlawed. Some men actually went bare except for a hanging cloak, though they carried their trousers over their shoulders like a burden. Others had made patchwork tartans from ragged scraps of cloth. A few wore their kilts, transformed into trousers by a few stitches between the legs. I quickly learned few spoke any English at all.

Finally when night fell, I came to a lone house where I asked for a bed. The owner professed no English and waved me away until I offered him one of my guineas. Then his English improved and he offered me a night's lodging. He promised to serve as a guide to Torosay.

The next day he accepted his money and tucked it away, then led me a little way past the house and pointed. Torosay lay right in front and I should use the hilltop for a landmark to

reach it. It was clear that was all the guidance I would get for my money.

After about an hour of walking, I came upon a ragged man who felt along the ground ahead of him with a stick as he walked. He was quite blind, he told me, but he was a teacher of the faith. I felt sure I was safe walking along with such a man.

He offered to be my guide to Torosay. "I know every stone and heather bush in the Isle of Mull," he said. Then he went on to point out landmarks all around us.

We had gone only a short way before I spotted the handle of a pistol under the flap of his coat. He began to ask me questions about myself. Was I from a rich family? Could I change a five-shilling piece for him?

All the while, he kept edging closer to me, and I kept stepping farther from him. As we walked, we looked like dancers instead of walkers.

The blind man grew angry and began to strike at my legs with his staff. That's when I told him

I had a pistol in my pocket too and if we didn't part company straightaway, I would blow his brains out.

He grudgingly turned at the bottom of the hill and disappeared into the next hollow. At Torosay, I found an innkeeper who spoke good English. He was delighted to find I could read and promptly spoke to me first in French, then Latin. His French was better than mine, but we were well matched in Latin.

He didn't recognize Breck's button but definitely knew the blind man from the road. "That is a very dangerous man," he said. "He has often been accused of highway robbery and once of murder."

Finally my landlord showed me to bed. I slept in good health and cheerier spirits than I'd had in many days.

There was a ferry from Torosay to Kinlochaline on the mainland. The skipper of the ferry was a clansman of Breck's and I was eager to speak with the man. But I had no chance when the ferry was loading.

We passed a dock where a single ship bobbed. It was packed with people. As we drew closer, we could hear the sound of crying and lamenting between the people of the ship and the people on the dock. I realized it must be a ship of exiles bound for the American colonies.

The travelers aboard our ferry began to sing a melancholy air that was quickly taken up by the emigrants and their friends on the beach. I saw tears running down faces all around me.

At Kinlochaline, I tugged the ferryman off to one side and showed him the button in the palm of my hand. "I'm seeking news of Alan Breck Stewart."

"Ah, I have word to see that you come safe," the man said. "But I suggest you not take your friend's name in your mouth again. It's not healthy to be overheard with it on your lips."

He quickly told me of a route that would take me to James of the Glens in Duror of Appin.

The man warned me to beware of Whigs and Campbells.

"Avoid the red coats and hide in the bush if any pass by," he urged.

I nodded agreement but saw no reason why I should be afraid of soldiers.

Early in my next day's journey, I overtook a serious little man dressed plainly in clerical style. He held a book before his nose as he walked. He explained that he was an evangelist, sent out to reach the more savage places of the Highlands. We soon struck up a lively conversation, and he reminded me greatly of my dear friend Mr. Campbell.

I asked him what he knew of the area. To my surprise, he eventually turned the conversation to Alan Breck.

"He is a bold, desperate customer," the minister said. "His life is forfeit already, so he'll shy away from nothing."

"You make a poor story of him," I said.

"Even Alan Breck is a man to be respected," the old man said. "He's loved here by many, and that's something to be said for any man. But, perhaps I have been too long in the Highlands?"

I told him I had seen much to admire in Highlanders as well. "After all, isn't Colin Campbell a Highlander?"

"Ay," he said. "And a fine blood. But he's put his head in the bees' nest now with trying to turn the clansmen off their land. It doesn't seem wise in my humble opinion."

"Do you think they'll fight?" I asked.

"Well, they're supposed to be disarmed," he said. "And Campbell will have soldiers. But I doubt his lady wife will rest easy until this is all done and he's home again."

We finally reached the door of the minister's dwelling. Before we went off to bed, he gave me a sixpence to help me on my journey. His generosity in the face of poverty overwhelmed me. I accepted the gift, for I knew of no gracious way to deny him.

CHAPTER 11

The Red Fox

The old minister found me a ride across
Linnhe Loch with a man who had a boat of
his own and planned to cross into Appin for
fishing. This saved me a long day's travel and
the price of two ferries.

We set out near noon. The day was cloudy
though the sun shone through small patches.
The sea was very deep and still. I actually put
water to my lips to see if it was truly salty.

Now and then the sun shone on moving
clumps of scarlet along the water side to the
north. My boatman said they were soldiers
marching from Fort William into Appin. It
was a sad sight to me, as I knew they would do
nothing good for these poor Highland people.

My boatman set me ashore at the edge of Loch Levin. I climbed through a wood of birches on the steep, craggy side of the mountain that overhung the loch. I found a spring and sat down to lunch upon the oat bread the minister had sent with me.

I wondered if I was doing the wise thing in seeking out Breck. Would I not be better off to go my own way? As I was sitting, I heard men and horses coming toward me through the wood.

Presently, I saw four travelers approaching. The first was a tall, redheaded man with a flushed face, who fanned himself with his hat. The second wore decent black clothes and a wig, and I felt sure this was a lawyer. The third was a servant. The man who rode fourth in line had the grim face of a sheriff's officer.

I rose and called out to the first man, asking the way to Aucharn. The men stopped and looked at me a little oddly.

"Do you suppose this is an omen?" the man asked the lawyer. "A young lad jumping out of the bracken to ask me about Aucharn."

"That is an ill subject for jesting," the lawyer said sternly.

"What seek you in Aucharn?" asked Colin Roy Campbell, for that is who he was.

"A man who lives there," I said.

"Oh? So James of the Glens is gathering his people?" the Red Fox said.

"I am neither of his people nor yours," I said. "I am an honest subject of King George."

"Very well said. Why is an honest man so far from his country?" Just as he spoke these words, the shot of a gun sounded from higher up the hill. Campbell fell upon the road. "Oh, I am dead!" he cried several times.

As his men gathered around him, I began to scramble up the hill to seek the murderer. I moved so quickly that when I reached the top of the hill, the murderer was still moving away at no great distance. He was a big man and carried a long gun.

"Here!" I shouted. "I see him."

At that, the murderer gave a little look over his shoulder and began to run. I ran after him until I heard someone behind me shout for me to halt. I looked back and saw soldiers gathered around the lawyer.

"Ten pounds to anyone who takes that lad," the lawyer said. "He's an accomplice to the killer."

The soldiers began to spread and still I stood, stunned.

"Duck in here among the trees," said a voice close by.

I hardly knew what I was doing, but I obeyed. As I did, a soldier shot through the bushes. I could hear the whistle of the bullet. Just inside the shelter of the trees, I found Alan Breck carrying a fishing rod.

"Come," he said as he set off running along the side of the mountain. Like a sheep, I followed him.

A quarter of an hour later, Alan stopped and dropped down flat in heather. "Do as I do," he whispered. My own sides ached and my head swam. My tongue hung out of my mouth with heat and dryness. I lay beside him like one dead.

Alan was the first to come round. "Well," he said, "that was a hot burst, David."

I said nothing. I had seen murder. A tall, cheerful gentleman was struck out of life in a moment. I knew how Breck felt about Campbell. But I knew also that I had seen the murderer and it wasn't Breck. Still, were the two men connected? I could not look upon his face.

"Are you still worn out?" he asked.

"No," I said. Then I took a deep breath and spoke my piece. "I like you very well, Alan, but your ways are not my ways. We should part."

"I'll not abandon you without some kind of reason," Breck said gravely.

"You know very well that Campbell man lies in his blood upon the road."

Breck was silent for little. Then he said, "If I had set out to rain revenge upon a Campbell, I believe I would carry a sword and a gun, not a fishing pole."

"That makes sense," I admitted.

"I swear I had no part in what you saw."

"I thank God for that." I offered him my hand. He seemed not to see it. "Did you know the man in the black coat?"

"I barely saw him," Breck said. "But I am sure his coat was blue. But then I have a grand memory for forgetting."

I realized then that Breck would play no part in catching the real murderer. His morals were topsy-turvy. "I'll not pretend I understand," I said, "but I'll offer you my hand again."

He took it then and shook it. He said we must flee the country as soon as possible. Every soldier would be looking for us.

"But we didn't do anything," I said. "I have nothing to fear from justice."

"The law does not work here as you know it," he said. "You and I would be arrested by Campbells, tried by Campbells, and convicted by Campbells. Then a Campbell would put the rope around our necks. We face no other future if we stay here."

That frightened me a little. It would have frightened me more had I known it was true.

"Take my word and run," he urged. "It is a hard thing to skulk and starve in the heather, but it's harder still to lie shackled in a red-coat prison waiting for the hangman."

He said we must head to the lowlands, but warned it would be a hard journey. We shook hands on it. Breck scouted back a bit to see what the soldiers were doing. It was clear they had lost our trail when he saw them hurrying along a trail in the wrong direction. Breck smiled as he watched them.

"We can sit down and eat a bite," Breck said. "They'll not be looking our way soon. We'll head to the house of James of the Glens. We can get clothes there and food."

While we ate, he told me about the shipwreck. Only the able-bodied men had made it to the skiff before the ship broke up. They had not been able to save the injured. As he described their screams, he shuddered.

The skiff reached the beach easily enough. He said Captain Hoseason called for the men to lay hands on him, but the other sailors had no interest in fighting. Riach stepped up to defend Breck if he needed and the captain lost interest in the fight.

The House of Fear

Night fell as we were walking, and the clouds settled thick and dark. We trekked across rough mountainside, and I could not see how Alan knew what direction to go.

At last we came to the top of a ridge and saw lights below us. A house door stood open and let out light. Around the house, five or six people moved hurriedly about carrying torches.

"James must have lost his wits," Breck said. "If we were soldiers, he would be in a fine mess." He whistled three times. At the first sound, all the torchlight froze. Then at the sound of the third whistle, the bustle began again.

We came down the hill to the yard gate. A tall, handsome man of about fifty stepped out of the shadows to greet us.

"James Stewart!" Breck cried out. "Meet my young friend from the lowlands. We'll give his name the go-by."

James of the Glens greeted me cordially and spoke in English when Breck told him I could not speak Gaelic. "There is great trouble coming for the country," he said gravely.

Breck shrugged. "You have to take the sour with the sweet. Colin Roy will do no more harm to our people."

"He'll do more harm in death than in life," Stewart said, shaking his head. "It's Appin that must pay for what happened. You know it."

While they talked, I looked around. Men on ladders dug in the thatch of the house and farm. They pulled out guns and swords and carried them away. Their faces reflected panic, and several times I saw men run into one another. Now and then Stewart would call out a command, but no one seemed to listen.

Then a lass came out of the house carrying a bundle. "What's the lassie have?" Breck asked.

"Your French clothes," Stewart said. "We must not be caught with them. We'll bury them with the weapons."

"Bury my clothes!" Breck said, alarm plain in his face. "No." He grabbed the packet and retired into the barn to change.

I followed Stewart into the house. He gestured for me to sit and joined me. He spoke hospitably but was clearly distracted, finally jumping up to pace the room. His wife sat by the fire and wept with her face in her hands.

This was all wretched to see, and I was glad when Breck returned. One of the other men gave me a change of clothes as well. They also gave us each a sword and pistols, then a bundle with a bag of oatmeal, a pan, and a bottle.

"I've no money to give you," Stewart said, though he had scraped together a few coppers. "Find a safe place and send word. Then, perhaps I can do more." His face paled. "If I don't hang."

"That would be a bad day for all of Appin," Breck said.

"After you leave," Stewart said, "I'll have to set a warrant for your arrest and for his too." He gestured to me.

Alan flushed. "I understand for me, but it makes me a traitor for bringing him here to be used this way."

"We'll not have his name," Stewart said, "just his look. You know I can't be seen to side with you, Alan."

Breck shook his head but turned to me. "What say you?"

"Write the warrant if you please," I said, assuming they would do it whether I liked it or not. "Write a warrant for King George too, as long as you're writing warrants for innocent men."

As soon as the words were out of my mouth, Mrs. Stewart leaped up and ran to me. She wept on my neck and on Breck, thanking us for letting the family protect itself this way.

"I'll keep your face in my heart," she said. "And I'll pray for you and bless you."

Thereupon we said farewell and set out again, heading east in the mild dark night. Sometimes we walked and sometimes we ran. We passed huts and houses hidden in quiet places of the hills. Breck stopped at every one to pass on the news so that the people might be prepared for the coming soldiers.

We ran past a rocky river whose horrid thundering made my belly quake. We reached a place where the river plunged into a falls, divided into three by huge rocks. Breck looked neither right nor left but jumped clean upon the first rock and I followed. Then he made a leap to the second. The flat space at the top was small, and he took care not to pitch off the far side. I followed him and he caught me.

We stood side by side with the last huge leap ahead of us. The roar of the water around us and the slippery rock terrified me. Breck leaped and reached the farther branch of the stream, landing safely.

I stood alone on the rock. Breck had made it. *I am younger, surely I can as well,* I thought. My shaky legs seemed ill fit for jumping. I bent low and flung myself forward with a kind of wild despair. I caught by my hands and was sliding back toward the roaring water when Breck grabbed me. He dragged me to safety.

We said not a word, but only set off running again. I stumbled as I ran, my legs still trembling from my near fall. A stitch in my side made me pant with the pain, but still I ran. When Breck finally paused under a great rock, it was none too soon for me.

I looked at the huge boulder and saw it was really two rocks leaning together. Breck called me to give him a boost so he could scramble up. Then he dangled his leather belt and I used that to help me make my own climb.

Where the rocks leaned together, they made a shallow dish that could have hidden three or four men. Breck looked around and finally smiled.

"Now we have a chance," he said. "You're going to think me a fool, David. I've let us come away with no water."

I offered to run back and fill the bottle with water from the river, but Breck shook his head. "There's no time. The soldiers will pass soon. Use this time to get some rest. I'll watch."

I lay down in a little peaty earth on top of the two rocks and fell hard asleep. I woke to find Breck's hand over my mouth.

"You were snoring," he whispered.

I looked confused and he gestured for me to peer over the side of the rock. The day had turned cloudless and hot. Camps of sentries were planted all around our hiding place.

"We're at a rough spot, David," Breck said. "But if we make it through the day, we might get by them in the night."

And so we lay on the bare rock. The sun beat upon us and heated the rock until we could hardly endure the touch of it. The peaty spot was cooler but would only hold one man at a time, so we took turns laying on it. The soldiers moved about the rock all day.

Finally the sun shifted to make a shady spot on the side of the rock farthest from the soldiers. "As well one death as another," Breck whispered and slipped over the edge of the rock to drop into the shadow.

I fell down beside him and we sat, completely exposed if any soldier cared to walk that way. None did. We began to slip from rock to rock, crawling on our bellies toward the river. The heat of the day had made the soldiers sleepy, and we spotted several dozing at their posts.

By sundown we had covered some distance with our crawling. We came to a deep, rushing stream and plunged head and shoulders into the water. I don't know which was better, the cold on our hot, blistered skin or the taste of the icy water.

We lay there until the water made our bones ache with chill. Then we made a dinner of cold water and oatmeal, which was enough for a hungry man.

In the shadow of night we set forth again. Now we could travel standing up and could walk with less fatigue. Breck grew so merry that he whistled, but I found myself wishing my adventures were over and I was home again.

CHAPTER 13

Flight

Though day comes early in the beginning of July, it was still dark when we reached the cleft in the head of a great mountain. A cave dipped into the rock there. A stream full of trout ran through the middle. Birches grew in a thin wood and the air was filled with birdsong.

The cleft was called Heaugh of Corrynakiegh. The five days we lived in it went happily. We slept in the cave on a bed of heather bushes. We made a fire so we could have hot porridge and grilled trout.

Breck tried to teach me to use a sword, but I found no real skill in it. Breck announced that we must send word to James Stewart. Since we were surrounded by only birds and trout, I could not imagine how we might do that.

Breck borrowed back the silver button he'd given me and strung it on a strip of greatcoat. He used the strip to bind a stick of birch to a stick of pine in a small cross.

"A little village lies near here. I have friends there, but there are a few I'm not so trusting of. I'll leave this in the window of a friend when it comes dark again so he'll know to come to us."

"And he'll understand what it means?"

"It's very like the sign for a clan gathering, but with my button so he'll know that it's me making the call. The birch and pine should guide him to the place where both birch and pine grow. It's not common."

"Wouldn't it be easier to write him a note?" I asked.

"Easier for me," he said. "But my friend never learned to read."

So Breck carried his cross away in the night. About noon the next day, a ragged man straggled up the open side of the mountain. Breck whistled to guide the man to us. The man wore a wild beard on his pockmarked face.

Breck wrote a note for the man to carry away to Stewart. He returned three days later, clearly pleased to be finished with his dangerous mission.

He told us the country was alive with red coats. Stewart and some of his servants were in prison at Fort William. The messenger had spoken to Stewart's wife and she had sent a bare bit of money and the handbill that described Breck and myself.

I was described as "a tall, strong lad of about eighteen with no beard," while Breck was called "a small, pockmarked, active man of thirty-five."

I realized it would be wiser for both of us if we traveled separately since there was little in the bill to make me stand out except for my being with Breck. When I suggested parting, Breck said he would never abandon me.

So we journeyed east across country colored red with heather. Peats and bogs dotted the land. A forest of dead firs stood like skeletons. With the land offering no hiding, we moved across it with care.

Sometimes we crawled from one heather bush to another. The rest of the time we walked stooping nearly to the knees.

We rested at noon and I fell asleep, though it was my turn at watch. When I jolted awake, a body of soldiers on horses were drawing near to us from the southeast.

I woke Breck and we ran on hands and knees toward the mountains. Hour upon hour we traveled this way. When night fell, Breck pushed on. It seemed we crawled and crept and dashed for an endless time. The next day's sun baked us and the awkward gait made my joints ache.

Finally we reached the foot of the mountain where we were ambushed by rough men. With a dirk at my throat, I was certain our time was done, but I was too exhausted to feel any fear at the thought of dying.

"These are Cluny's men," Breck crowed. "We could not have fallen upon better."

My strength was gone. I had to be half carried through a maze of dreary glens and hollows and into the heart of that dismal mountain of Ben Alder.

Cluny's Cage

Finally we reached the strange house that was known in the country as "Cluny's Cage." The trunks of several trees had been used as corner posts with walls between formed from stakes pounded into the ground. Another tree grew nearly sideways from the hillside and made the center beam of the roof.

The house was such an odd combination of nature and workmanship that it looked a bit like a giant wasp's nest in the hillside thicket. It was large enough to shelter five or six people in comfort. A projection from the cliff formed a chimney and smoke drifted up, blending with the rock face.

Cluny greeted us warmly. It was clear that he found the life of hiding lonely. He certainly seemed delighted by our company and the opportunity for news.

After we ate, Cluny brought out a pack of cards and suggested we play. I had been raised to believe card playing was the worst kind of sin. As I had a bit of a fever and little enough sense, I said as much.

"What kind of talk is that in the house of Cluny Macpherson?" the offended man demanded.

Breck spoke up for me calmly, but added, "I don't think the lad is well. He should rest, and I will play any game you care to name."

I stumbled to a bed of heather in the corner and was soon asleep. I would sleep and wake and sleep and wake for several days. I raved with fever and a doctor of sorts was fetched to peer at me. During all this time, Cluny and Breck played hand after hand of cards.

At one point, Breck knelt over me and asked for the loan of some money. I stared at him, thinking his eyes were strangely big. His nose alarmed me as if he might be a bird who would peck at me. I told him to take whatever he liked, then fell asleep again.

On the morning of the third day, I awoke without fever.

"My scouts report all clear to the south," Cluny said. "Do you have the strength to go?"

"I don't know if I'm as well as I should be," I said, then glanced at Breck to see what he thought.

He looked at me guiltily. "I've lost all our money, David. That's the truth of it."

"My money, too?" I asked.

He nodded glumly, but Cluny just laughed. "Of course you'll have your money back and more besides. I'd not send you out without money. The cards were for the joy of it and for the company."

He insisted we take a well-stocked purse, but I was deeply angry with Breck for having run such a risk with what little we had. We set out without my speaking to him again.

It was clear soon enough that I wasn't fit for the long, hard slog ahead. But I kept pressing onward, nursing my anger at my friend.

The weather turned wet and cold, and still we walked. Breck apologized many times, but I had no interest in accepting. Finally, he seemed to decide he had suffered enough. He stopped begging my forgiveness and went along whistling cheerfully.

I was exhausted and ached from shivering. The chill wind cut through me and the teasing cheerfulness of Breck seemed to rub against me harder and harder. Finally I turned on him as he was singing a cheerful battle song.

"Why do you choose that song?" I asked. "Doesn't it remind you that you and your people have been nothing but beaten?"

Breck looked at me in stunned silence for a moment. "Do you know that you insult me?" he asked softly.

"Then I am ready to respond," I said, clumsily pulling my sword.

"Are you daft?" Breck asked. "I can't fight you, David. It would be murder."

"What problem have you with murder?" I asked, waving my sword like the young fool I was.

Breck drew his sword, but before his blade could touch mine, he threw it away and fell to the ground. "No, I cannot. I cannot."

At that, my anger and the little strength it gave me slipped away. My knees buckled and I said, "Alan, if you cannot help me, I must die on my own."

He hurried to my side. "I'll help you. We'll get you to a house to rest." He helped me to my feet and took much of my weight as we stumbled along. "I should have seen you were dying on your feet. What kind of man am I?"

"Neither of us is better than the other," I said, leaning on my friend. "You're good to me."

Breck knocked at the first door we reached and chance served us well. The kind people gave me a place to rest and heal. I stayed a full month so that we might take to the road in full health.

The End of Our Flight

My time of healing was uneventful except for a surprise visit I had from Robin Oig, the son of the notorious Rob Roy. The young man had shot James MacLaren in a quarrel never settled. Now he walked into the house of his blood enemies as if it were an inn.

He introduced himself to me as I lay in bed. I was thankful Alan Breck was out on some errand, for I suspected their meeting would not be pleasant.

Robin Oig told me his family owed a debt to the kin of Balfour of Baith. They had a kindness done by them in a time of battle.

I admitted I knew little of my family line. Oig stormed off, muttering about going to so much trouble for a kinless loon who didn't know his own father. As Oig reached the door, Breck opened it to come in.

The two men stared at one another. "Mister Stewart, I am thinking," Oig said.

"True," Breck said. "And not a name to be ashamed of."

Our host rushed between the men as each reached toward the hilt of his sword. "Gentlemen," he said, "I have two pipes, and you are each acclaimed pipers. I would love to see which of you is best."

"Why, sir," Breck said, having not shifted his eyes from Oig. "Are you a bit of a piper?"

"I am," Oig said.

Our host hurried to bring out the pipes. The two enemies sat down. Oig first played a little spring in a very bright manner.

"Aye, you can blow," Breck said. He responded by playing the same tune but decorated with grace notes that pipers love and call the "warblers."

"Not bad, Mr. Stewart," Oig said. Then he took up his pipes and proceeded to imitate and correct some part of Breck's variations, which he seemed to remember perfectly.

"Aye, you have music," Breck said gloomily. "You can blow the pipes, make the most of that."

Then Oig launched into a slow tune that was a special favorite of the Appin Stewarts. And any sign of anger in the men seem to flow away with the sweet, sad tune.

"Robin Oig," Breck said when it was done, "you are a great piper. I am not fit to blow in the same kingdom as you." Thus the quarrel was ended.

By the time I was well, we were nearly through August and the weather was beautiful and warm. The travel was easy, and I felt cheered to know we were so close to home.

Finally, Alan said, "We're in your own land again. We passed the Highlands line. Now if we can just get across that crooked water, we might throw our bonnets in the air."

A bridge crossed the water, but we soon saw it was heavily guarded. We had to find a boat if we were to hope to reach home again. I stared across the water knowing if I could just cross it, I could reach the lawyer Rankeillor and settle with my uncle.

We walked to a small merchant shop and bought bread and cheese. As we carried it outside to eat, Breck asked me, "Did you notice the lass we bought this from?"

"A bonny lass she was," I answered.

"She noticed you too," he said. "I believe that might get us a boat."

"I don't think I look that good," I said.

"I don't want her to fall in love with you," he said with a laugh. "I want her to feel sorry for you. There's no end of good that can come from the good-hearted lass who feels sorry for you."

Breck dragged me back to the merchant where we played up my recent illness and my pining to cross the river and be home again before I died. He made me sound so woeful I almost took a fever at the sound of it.

"Has he no friends?" she said tearfully.

"Aye, but all on the other side," Breck said. "And no way to reach them."

"If only I could reach Mr. Rankeillor of Ferry."

"Rankeillor the lawyer?" she asked, clearly assuming he was one of the friends Breck had spoken of.

At this the lass turned and ran out of that part of the house, leaving us alone. I groaned at the deceit my friend had poured out, but just as I did, the lass came back.

"Poor lamb!" she said, setting food before us. "You can trust me. I'll find a way to put you over."

At evening, the lass herself rowed us across the river. She waved away thanks, shook our hands, and set immediately forth for her own side again. I looked around on the shore. I was nearly home.

Mr. Rankeillor

When light came, we decided Alan Breck would fend for himself until sunset while I contacted Mr. Rankeillor. Then we would meet again.

I hurried into Queen's Ferry. As I strode down the street, I was struck suddenly with my own appearance. Would Mr. Rankeillor even see me? I was dressed in Highland rags and was filthy from hair to feet.

I passed gentlemen in the street, but couldn't muster up the courage to speak to them, looking as I did. I noticed a dog sitting on a step of a home that reminded me of my father's. I suddenly felt more sharply homesick than at any moment before.

The door of the home fell open and a kindly man in a well-powdered wig and spectacles stepped out. He took one look at me and walked quickly up to ask if I were in need. I told him I was looking for the home of Mr. Rankeillor.

"This is his house," he said. "And I am that very man."

"My name is David Balfour," I said, nearly weak in the knees to know I had reached my destination. "I have come from many strange places of late. I would like to tell you more in a private manner."

"I have heard your name." He led me back to the house and quizzed me about my parents and life in Essendean. "Did you ever meet a man of the name of Hoseason?" he asked finally.

I stared in wonder, then told him of my uncle's plan and the part Captain Hoseason had played in it.

Mr. Rankeillor told me that my dear friend Mr. Campbell had stormed into his office on the very day of my shipwreck. He had demanded that the lawyer find me.

"I have interviewed many people and heard many stories since," the lawyer said. "Your uncle told Mr. Campbell that you left on the ship to seek your fortune at sea willingly. Mr. Campbell did not believe him. Captain Hoseason said you drowned in an accident at sea. So you see, I have heard many stories, including yours."

I thought about this for a moment and said, "If we enlist the help of a friend, I believe we can hear the true story. But my friend's identity will have to remain secret."

I hinted enough at Breck's past that Mr. Rankeillor agreed that it would be best to speak of it no more. Mr. Rankeillor had his servants draw me a bath and loaned me some of his own son's clothes.

That evening we collected Breck. As we walked, I mused about my uncle's cruelty. Mr. Rankeillor told me the story of my father and his brother.

It seemed Uncle Ebenezer was a very popular young man and a bit spoiled by his older brother. Both brothers fell in love with the same lady and she chose Alexander. Uncle Ebenezer threw himself in bed, claiming he would die from his broken heart.

At the end, my father told his young brother that he would give him the whole of the estate and leave with his young bride. But he left so suddenly, the stories cropped up. Many believed Ebenezer had killed his brother. He was shunned and turned into a cold-hearted hermit. The fine house fell to ruin.

"But the estate is yours beyond a doubt," the lawyer said. "It doesn't matter what the brothers said between themselves."

"I don't really want the estate," I said. "I only want enough to make my own way, and I believe my plan will allow that to happen without courts or trials."

Breck went along easily enough with my plan. It was quite dark when we arrived at the house

of Shaws. The lawyer and I kept to the shadows while Breck pounded on the door. Eventually my uncle poked his head and his blunderbuss out the window and demanded quiet.

"I am here for your good, Mr. Balfour," Breck said. "Some friends of mine have found your nephew cast ashore on the Isle of Mull. They'll return him safely to you for a bit of thanks."

Uncle Ebenezer cried out for him to be quiet, then rushed down to speak through the open kitchen door. "My nephew wasn't a good lad at the best of it, and I'll offer no money to get him back."

Breck shrugged. "You'd not be very popular if folks knew you wouldn't pay to help your brother's son."

My uncle sniffed. "I'm not very popular in the countryside now."

"Well, if you'll not pay us to give him back," Breck said. "Will you pay us to keep him? What do you want done with him and what will you pay to see it?"

My uncle didn't answer, but shifted uneasily. "Let me think on it."

"Let's deal plainly," Breck said. "Do you want the boy killed or kept?"

"Kept, kept. I want no bloodshed."

"That will cost you," Breck said. "There's so much trouble with keeping a lad. You have to feed him and put clothes on him. He's a big one, you know."

"Still, I'll not have him killed," the old man said.

"Then I'll have what you paid Hoseason for kidnapping him," Breck said.

"That's a lie!"

"Hoseason and I are partners," Breck said. "He says it's true. Shall we bring the boy back and see what he says?"

"Well, I don't know what Hoseason says, but I only gave him twenty pounds. He said he would make more money when he sold the boy in the Carolinas."

"Thank you," Mr. Rankeillor said as he stepped from the shadows. "And good evening, Mr. Balfour."

I stepped out then too and added, "Good evening, Uncle Ebenezer."

All the fight went out of my uncle then. He knew I could have everything with his confession, so it was easy enough to get him to agree to terms.

My uncle would stay on the land and pay me two-thirds of the yearly income. The money would be paid to Mr. Rankeillor to help avoid any more accidents. So my adventure had taken me from a poor man's son to a man of means.

I still felt I owed so much to Breck. Mr. Rankeillor told me sadly that there was really nothing he could do to help the trial of James Stewart or in getting the warrant lifted for Alan Breck. Breck took the news cheerily enough.

"I didn't have much thought of help in that," he said. "I'll be on my way."

I gave Breck the money Mr. Rankeillor had advanced me. We found a ship to take him safely away.

"Well, good-bye," Breck said, holding out his hand.

"Good-bye," I said, grasping his hand in return. We turned away from each other then, and I could have sat down by the dyke and cried like a baby. I walked into the town and let the crowd carry me to and fro.

Finally I found myself standing before the very doors of the British Linen Company's bank. There, Mr. Rankeillor had secured me a line of credit while details of my share of the estate were worked out.

So I walked up the stairs to my new life.